Dogs Don't Do DISHES

REBECCA LISLE

Illustrated by Tim Archbold

Andersen Press · London

For Gemma and Florence (R.L.)

First published in 2004 by
Andersen Press Limited,
20 Vauxhall Bridge Road, London SW1V 2SA
www.andersenpress.co.uk

British Library Cataloguing in Publication Data
available
ISBN 1 84270 314 5

Phototypeset by Intype Libra Ltd
Printed and bound in Great Britain by
Mackays of Chatham Ltd.,
Chatham, Kent

1
The Junior Inventor's First Invention

Tom and the black and white dog walked down the long corridor.

Tom was nervous. So nervous, he was hiccuping and his hiccups were bouncing off the big glass windows and steel walls of the Institute of Inventions, like the cries of a giant, sad frog.

The noise made the dog wince. The Junior Inventor shouldn't be *that* nervous.

'Nearly there, hic,' whispered Tom.

And I wish we weren't, thought the dog.

They stopped at the massive grey door marked BOSSES. Tom put down his cleaning things, straightened his tie, picked a speck of dust off his

trousers, smoothed down his hair, smoothed the dog's fur.

'Metal-Mutt,' he said. 'This – is – it.'

The dog wagged his tail. Yep! This is it!

Metal-Mutt looked like an ordinary dog with floppy black ears, a waggy tail and a wet black nose. He even smelt like an ordinary dog, but he was not ordinary, he was Tom's *fantastic* invention.

Tom knocked on the Bosses' door.

The door swung silently open on well-oiled hinges. Tom cleared his throat. Metal-Mutt cleared his.

Here goes! they both thought and went in.

The room was enormous and completely empty, except for a massive desk at the far end, behind which the three bosses sat, staring at them through black glasses.

'Mood gorning. Whoops! Gord mooning. No. Er, *good morning*,' said

Tom, bobbing up and down.

Oh, kiss a cat! thought Metal-Mutt.
Tom's scared speechless.

'Ten thirty,' said the first boss,
looking at the papers on his desk.
'Tom Brigg. Dog invention.'

'Dogs have already been invented,'
said the second boss.

'Yes, yes, but this is Metal-Mutt,' said the Junior Inventor. 'This isn't a *real* dog.'

Metal-Mutt smiled up at the three bosses and wagged his tail: but I wish I was!

'Go on,' said boss number three, darkly.

'Well, everyone wants a clean and tidy house,' Tom said, 'don't they? But nobody likes doing the housework, do they?' He tried to smile but it was hard to smile at the three stony faces. 'And,' went on the Junior Inventor, 'most people can't afford a cleaner, so, I've invented a dog which cooks and cleans.'

Metal-Mutt snapped lazily at a passing bluebottle and flicked his ears. That's me!

The three bosses stared back blankly. It was impossible to know what went on behind the black glasses, but whatever it was, Metal-Mutt didn't get the feeling it was good.

'Dogs don't do dishes,' said boss number one.

'Er, this one does,' said Tom. 'Go on, Metal-Mutt, show them what you can do.'

2
Metal-Mutt, the Cleaning Machine

Metal-Mutt wagged his tail. He wanted to do well for the Junior Inventor, even though cleaning wasn't *really* his idea of fun.

So he began with polishing. He shook the aerosol can then sprayed polish liberally over the big wooden desk. Using a fresh yellow duster from the bucket, he rubbed the desk vigorously.

'Stop!' said the first boss.

What did I do wrong? Metal-Mutt wondered. He scratched his ears and yawned. He did want to please. Maybe I should run round and round chasing my tail? That's fun to watch and fun to do.

'Better show them how you do the

windows,' whispered Tom.

They were both proud of Metal-Mutt's window cleaning. He never left any smears on the glass, but he'd hardly begun before . . .

'Stop,' said boss number two.

Metal-Mutt shivered. What's wrong? Why don't they like me? Perhaps I should bark. He glanced up at Tom.

'Hoover,' hissed Tom.

Metal-Mutt plugged in the hoover quickly. The motor sounded very loud and harsh in the empty room.

'No!' snapped the third boss. 'Make him stop. STOP!'

'But, you've hardly seen anything yet!' cried Tom, desperately scanning his list. 'He can cook and sew and wash up and . . .'

'No,' said boss number one.

He put a large cross against Metal-Mutt's name.

'Why?' cried the Junior Inventor. 'He's a wonderful invention.'

'I don't like dogs,' said boss number two. 'They bite.'

He put a cross against Metal-Mutt's name as well.

'If everyone had a Metal-Mutt, cleaners would be put out of business. And what would my wife do all day? No,' said boss number three, putting a cross on the paper. 'Absolutely no!'

The three bosses folded their arms on the desk. Their black glasses looked blankly at Tom and Metal-Mutt.

'He must be destroyed immediately,' said boss number one.

'Invent something useful,' said boss number two.

'Leave the room,' said boss number three.

And that was that.

Tom knew that since he was only a Junior Inventor, the very youngest in the Institute, there was no point in arguing.

Metal-Mutt gazed up at him sadly. I knew I should have barked a bit, he thought.

3
Only One Remaining

The Junior Inventor took Metal-Mutt back to his laboratory.

'I'm sorry,' he said, stroking Metal-Mutt's soft, floppy ears. 'What shall we do? I can't take you home, I'm not allowed pets where I live . . .' He paced up and down. 'I could never destroy you . . . I know! I'll put an advertisement in the corner shop. Someone must want a cooking, cleaning, jolly dog like you.'

'Woof,' agreed Metal-Mutt, because more than anything, Metal-Mutt wanted a proper home to look after, one with children, near a park, oh, that would be a dream come true!

Tom wrote out his advertisement neatly on a postcard.

METAL-MUTT
WOMAN'S BEST FRIEND
Metal-Mutt will keep your house
clean and tidy for you.
No more ironing! No more
cooking! No more washing!
He looks just like a real dog but
he's a cleaning machine!
A must for every home.
ONE ONLY REMAINING

Tom thought 'one only remaining' gave the ad an authentic touch.

It was 3.32 when he reached the corner shop.

'That sounds a nice sort of dog to have,' said Mrs Juggins, reading the postcard thoughtfully. 'If we didn't have our cat, Arthur, I'd take him.'

'Oh, Mrs Juggins, I wish you could. He'd be happy with you.'

'But he'd hate Arthur,' said Mrs Juggins, grinning. 'Everyone does.'

At 3.35, little Cherise Orchard
stopped at the corner shop on her way
back from school. She read the
advertisement carefully.

'Oh!'

Then she read it all the way through
again, very slowly, in a loud whisper.
As she got near the end, her heart was
thumping excitedly in her chest.

'Perfect! I so want a dog! Mum so wants help! This is just what we need all rolled into one! Oh, but how will I remember the address?'

She stared hard at the postcard and tried to memorise every word but there were a lot of words to remember.

At 3.40, a large solid girl arrived and pushed rudely in front of Cherise. It was Cindy Crumm, on her way back from school.

Cindy read the advertisement too.

'Fantastic!' she breathed, wiping her grubby hands down her grubby tee shirt. 'Brilliant. Just what we want.'

She looked down at Cherise, suspiciously. Had Cherise read it?

'Push off,' Cindy said gruffly.

Cherise pushed off. She ran all the way home to tell her mum.

Cindy had to act fast, she was sure Cherise had been thinking exactly the same as her. She went into the shop and asked Mrs Juggins for a tin of

peeled prawns. They were on the
highest shelf, and Mrs Juggins had to
climb up a ladder to reach them. When
she was wobbling about at the top,

Cindy pulled the postcard out from the window and stuffed it up her jumper.

It was 3.42.

There, now no one else would ever see the ad! The cleaning dog was as good as hers!

Arthur, the shop cat, glowered at her crossly from the counter.

Cindy said: 'Grrr!' right in his ear and Arthur fled.

4
The Crummy Crumms

When Cindy Crumm got home, she found her mum reclining on the sofa eating toffees. Her hair was in curlers. She was leafing through some catalogues: *Home Delivery Instant TV Dinners, Microwave Magic* and *Super Snappy Snacks.*

Mrs Crumm never cooked real food. She bought ready-made meals and heated them up in the microwave and just to make absolutely sure she never had to do any work, she used throw-away paper plates.

'This house is such a mess!' cried Cindy, flinging her school bag on the floor and kicking off her shoes. 'I wish it was nice and tidy.'

'So do I,' said her brother, Cyril.

'So do I,' said Mum.

'So do I,' said Dad, coming in from work. 'Why isn't there the delicious aroma of steak and kidney pie wafting through the house?'

''Cos I haven't opened the packet yet,' said Mrs Crumm and they all laughed.

They were a lazy lot.

'Take a look at this,' said Cindy, waving Tom's advertisement at them. 'The answer to our prayers.'

Mrs Crumm read the postcard.

'A *dog*? We don't want a smelly dog in the house!'

'Dogs are flea-bags!' said Cyril.

'But this one does the housework,' said Cindy. 'It'll cook dinners and everything. I want proper food like my friends.'

'Oh, go on,' said Mrs Crumm, reading the advertisement again. 'It can't.'

'I wouldn't mind having a look,' Mr

Crumm said. 'I mean, if it really did
those things . . . and if it wasn't too
expensive, why not?'

There was nothing to stop Mrs Crumm from cleaning the house, she was just too lazy. Cindy could have done some. There was nothing to stop Cyril from doing the housework either, or Mr Crumm, but they thought it was women's work. They could have afforded a cleaner, but they were too mean.

While the Crumm family were discussing Metal-Mutt, poor Cherise was rushing back to Mrs Juggins's shop to write down the address of the Institute of Inventions, because somehow she'd forgotten it. But by then, the postcard had gone.

5
Metal-Mutt Meets His New Family

Meanwhile Metal-Mutt had been hiding in the Junior Inventor's laboratory.

'I can't do this much longer,' Tom fretted, pushing Metal-Mutt under the desk.

Nor can I, thought Metal-Mutt.

'If they find you they'll fire me . . . You know, I really can't understand why no one has replied to my advertisement. I thought people would have been queuing up to buy you.'

It was *four* days since Tom had put the advertisement in the window, but the Crumms never did anything in a hurry. Now, at last, they were on their way.

They arrived at the Institute of

Inventions and were whooshed
upstairs in a rocket-like lift and shown
into Tom's laboratory.

The Crumm family huddled

together and shivered uncomfortably. The place was spotless; gleaming metal shelves, a squeaky clean floor and sparkling glass windows.

'It's like being in hospital,' whispered Cyril. 'Horrid.'

'We've come about your dog,' said Mr Crumm.

'The one that does housework,' said Mrs Crumm.

'Er, yes,' said Tom. He didn't want Metal-Mutt to go to *this* family: they didn't look . . . nice.

'Well, where is it then?' said Cindy.

'Or was it all a joke?' asked Mrs Crumm.

'I knew it was too good to be true,' said Mr Crumm. 'Nobody could make a dog do dishes.'

'No, no it is true,' said Tom. 'He is the most marvellous invention in the world, but . . . Oh well, I'd better show you, I suppose.' He pulled his chair out from his desk where Metal-Mutt was hiding. 'Out you come!'

Metal-Mutt rushed up to the Crumm family barking happily.

He licked the toffee off Mrs Crumm's hand.

'Ugh, disgusting,' yelped Mrs Crumm.

He sniffed Mr Crumm's smelly bits.

'Hey, mind your manners!' snapped Mr Crumm.

A family! A family of my very own, thought Metal-Mutt, happily. I'll lick you and take you for walks and bring back your sticks and – oh! lovely, lovely children!

He bounced at Cyril making him shriek like a kettle and jumped at Cindy so she wailed like a siren.

'He's just rather friendly,' said Tom, sadly.

'That's never a cleaning machine!' cried Cyril, dusting off the dog hairs. 'It's not made of metal!'

'You've tricked us,' cried Mrs Crumm, backing away. 'That's a real dog!'

'And it'll make a real mess,' said Mr Crumm.

'No, no,' explained Tom. 'It's not a real dog, well, only partly.'

Cyril poked Metal-Mutt. 'Are you sure?'

Cindy tried to pull his whiskers. 'It's got real whiskers.'

Metal-Mutt wagged his tail. 'Woof.'

'He looks just like a real dog,' said Tom, 'because I am a genius, but I assure you he is not. He's very special. Watch. Mutt, sweep the room, please!'

Metal-Mutt immediately picked up the broom and skipped round sweeping energetically.

'Ooooo, will you look at that!' cried Mrs Crumm.

'Mutt, show them how you do the ironing, please,' said Tom.

Metal-Mutt set up the ironing board, plugged in the iron and began to iron a white shirt with quiet determination.

'My, oh, my!' breathed Mrs Crumm. How glorious her home would be with freshly ironed sheets, real cakes, a carpet with no crumbs on it (well, Crumms, but not Crumbs, she giggled to herself). Wouldn't her neighbours be impressed! She'd be able to host Super Snappy Snack Parties, too.

Mr Crumm imagined his car getting
polished each week, the rubbish

cleared from the basement, his garage clean, and floating over this blissful picture was the aroma of steaming hot steak and kidney pie.

'We'll have it,' he said, getting out his wallet.

They want me! thought Metal-Mutt. Wag, wag, wag, went his tail. I'm going to a real home!

'You're very lucky,' Tom told them miserably. 'I wish I didn't have to let him go . . .'

'But you do,' said Mr Crumm, sharply.

Tom winced. 'Just remember,' he told them, 'although Metal-Mutt is made of metal and microchips, he has a dog's heart. He needs to be walked and played with just like all dogs do.'

'Yeah, yeah, yeah,' said Mr Crumm, unfolding a grubby wodge of notes. 'Sure. Treat him like a dog.'

6
Home Sweet Home

'I've always wanted a clean house,' said Mrs Crumm as they walked home.

'I've always wanted a proper dinner when I come home from work,' said Mr Crumm.

And I've always wanted to be a real dog, thought Metal-Mutt, peeing against a lamppost. He sniffed a dustbin and stuffed his nose into an empty burger box. His hackles shot up when a black cat hissed at him. I'm so happy!

'He's so lifelike!' cooed Mrs Crumm. 'But I'm glad he's not. I mean, I'd be scared of a real dog.'

'I still can't hardly believe it,' said Mr Crumm.

'This is where we live, Metal-Mutt,'

said Cindy, opening the door of 28 Iydal Avenue. 'Home.'

The Crumm family charged inside leaving Metal-Mutt on the doorstep. He followed them gingerly, stepping over the newspapers, apple cores, dirty clothes and shoes. In the kitchen his paws stuck to the tacky floor.

What a MESS!

He poked his nose into the fridge. Yuk! What a stink!

'Home, sweet home,' grinned Mrs Crumm. 'It's all yours, Mutt.'

The Crumm family sat down and turned on the television.

'Get on with it then!' snapped Mrs Crumm. 'Do what you're supposed to do. Clean the house first, then I want tea at seven, three courses, mind, and no sticking your paws in it!'

They all laughed.

Metal-Mutt tried to wag his tail but it felt very heavy all of a sudden, like his heart.

He went slowly upstairs.

Oh, what a stinky place the bathroom was! Metal-Mutt put a clothes peg on his nose and started to scrub the bath. There was toothpaste on the mirror, wet towels on the floor, stains on the walls. It took ages, but when he'd finished the bathroom was

gleaming, the toothbrushes were lined up neatly and even the rubber ducks looked happy.

Next he went into the bedrooms.

Horrible!

He picked all the clothes off the floor and put them into the dirty clothes basket. He changed the beds, he dusted and hoovered. Phew, it was hard work.

When he'd finished upstairs, he went downstairs and began cleaning there.

'This is fantastic!' said Mrs Crumm, lying back in her armchair so the dog could hoover under her feet. 'Great.'

'Here, Mutt,' said Mr Crumm, giving the dog his empty glass and plate. 'Take them to the kitchen, oh, and this, and this and this.' He piled so many things into Metal-Mutt's arms, he could hardly see where he was going. Everything wobbled as he staggered into the kitchen.

Mr Crumm roared with laughter.

Then Metal-Mutt had to prepare supper.

Nobody helped him, they left him alone in the kitchen to get on with it.

If they had gone in to lend a hand or even just to show him where the spoons were kept, they would have

seen Metal-Mutt sitting on a stool with
his apron over his head.

He was crying.

7
Dogsbody

Nobody's patted my head once,
sobbed Metal-Mutt. Nobody's said
'good boy' or rubbed my ears or
anything . . . Oh, Tom, how could you
do this to me?

'Tea at seven, don't forget!' shouted
Mrs Crumm above the roar of the
television, and Metal-Mutt jumped up
and got to work.

I wish I couldn't do all these clever
things, thought Metal-Mutt, rolling
out pastry. I wish I was just an
ordinary dog and they were an
ordinary family who'd take me to the
park.

Metal-Mutt cooked delicious meat
pies shaped like bones to remind the
Crumms he really was a dog. For

pudding, he made a ring-shaped cake
and decorated it like a dog's collar. He
was looking forward to wearing a
collar.

When it was ready he rang a bell to
call them in to eat.

'My, look at this!' laughed Mr
Crumm, staring at the table. 'It's a
dog's dinner!'

'Not bad,' said Mrs Crumm.
'Almost as good as *Microwave Magic*.'

'And no washing up,' said Cindy.

'Yeah! No clearing up! Well done for seeing that advert, Cindy!' cried Cyril.

Metal-Mutt sat in the corner and watched them eat and when they'd finished and left the kitchen, he quietly ate up the unwanted scraps.

Next day was Sunday. Metal-Mutt got up early and swept the floors, dusted and polished, and cleaned out the fridge. He ran down to the nearest shop and collected the newspaper. He put the washing on and he baked croissants for breakfast.

When it was time for the family to get up, Metal-Mutt took tea up to everyone. He drew back the curtains and let the sun shine in. He desperately wanted to say:

'Come on! It's a lovely day for the park!'

But he couldn't speak.

The Crumm family got up slowly, groaning and grumbling. They rolled

downstairs groaning and grumbling.

'Wow!' cooed Mrs Crumm, looking round. 'I thought that dog was a dream, but it's true! The whole house is gleaming!'

'Spotless,' said Mr Crumm, munching a croissant and carelessly

letting the crumbs drop on the floor.
'He's our very own dogsbody!'

'I like it clean,' said Cindy,
splattering hot chocolate all over her
clean tee shirt.

Metal-Mutt doggedly prepared the
Sunday lunch while Mr and Mrs
Crumm watched TV and the children
played on the computer.

He stood on a chair at the kitchen sink, peeling the potatoes and gazing through the window at the park. There were lots of people in the park. A big Dalmatian was pulling a small boy along on his skateboard.

That looks jolly, thought Metal-Mutt.

A puppy was splashing after a duck in the river.

I'd love to do that, thought Metal-Mutt.

A spaniel yapped and skipped, waiting for two little girls to throw him a ball.

That looks fun, he thought, and a tear splashed into the potato water. That park really does look fun.

Why, oh, why did Tom give me the heart and feelings of a real dog?

8
Metal-Mutt Begins to Despair

Day after day, Metal-Mutt cleaned and
scrubbed, mended, polished and
shopped.

Once, Cindy said 'thank you' to
him.

Once, Cyril patted his head, but then said: 'Oh, what do you care? You're only a machine.'

Metal-Mutt waited patiently to be taken out for a walk. He sat by the back door. He sat by the front door. He even tied Mr Crumm's tie round his neck as a hint, but they still didn't take him out.

He slept on the kitchen floor.

He ate the Crumms' leftovers.

He spent hour after hour alone.

Metal-Mutt's nose became dry. He lost weight. His fur didn't gleam anymore.

Then, at last, something happened to change everything.

9
Metal-Mutt Goes for a Swim

It happened on a Saturday.

After a busy morning polishing the brass on the front door and the silver teaspoons Mrs Crumm had inherited from her mother; cleaning and polishing all the shoes (including washing and ironing the laces), *and* doing Cyril's homework, Metal-Mutt sank down in the sunshine and closed his eyes . . .

'MUTT!' Mrs Crumm yelled. 'The washing's finished. Hang it up in the sun quick, before it all creases.'

Metal-Mutt staggered outside with the basket of wet clothes. His nose twitched, smelling the breeze, rich with the glorious scents of dog, cat, rat and bones. Mmm, lovely!

A real metal machine wouldn't mind
doing all the chores, thought Metal-
Mutt, pegging up a sheet. Or not being
loved. A real machine would just do it.
But I want to be a real dog and dogs
don't hang up washing!

He stared across to the park, the trees, the pond, while he absent-mindedly pinned a blue shirt to the line . . .

'Help! Help!'

Who was that?

Metal-Mutt dropped the washing and ran to the end of the garden. On the other side of the fence, just twenty metres away, was the park and river. There, clutching an overhanging branch, dangling above the fast-flowing water, was a little girl.

'Help!'

Her teddy bear had fallen in the water and she was trying to reach it, but any minute now . . .

SPLASH!

The girl tumbled in and went right under. Then she bobbed up, gasping for breath.

'Help!'

The fast current whisked her away down the river.

Metal-Mutt didn't hesitate. He bounded over the fence, dived into the water and began swimming after the little girl as fast as he could.

Metal-Mutt's legs already ached from going up and down the stairs, but he swam. His paws were sore from ironing and polishing, even his metal brain box was hurting from Cyril's homework, but on he swam.

I must get her. Can't stop. Must reach her.

The girl's mother shouted from the grass bank. 'I can't swim! Save her, please! Help!'

The girl was sinking, just the top of her head was showing like a bit of brown seaweed. Metal-Mutt made a mighty effort and surged forward. He grabbed her collar and yanked her face clear of the water.

'Waagh!' cried the girl, taking a breath.

Metal-Mutt pulled the girl safely

onto the bank, then collapsed.

Oh, my legs! he moaned. He shook his head. Feels like there's a mad bee in my head. Oh, my heart! Thump, thump thump, like a drum! I'm going to die!

He lay beside the girl, panting and dripping.

The mother soon reached them and took the girl in her arms.

'Darling! Cherise!' she crooned. 'You're safe.' She turned to Metal-Mutt. 'Good dog!' she said. 'Well done, boy!'

Metal-Mutt froze. *What*?

'Good boy,' the mother said again, reaching out and patting his head. 'Thank you so much!'

That was it! It was those glorious words which Metal-Mutt had been longing to hear.

'*Good boy*.' Something melted inside him, flooding through him like liquid chocolate, sweet and delicious.

'*Good dog.*'

'Cherise, Cherise.' The mother squeezed the little girl. 'Is she all right?'

Isn't she? Metal-Mutt jumped and licked Cherise's face, her ears, her chin, every bit he could reach. Not everyone would like to be licked so thoroughly by a wet dog, but this little girl didn't mind at all and nor did her mother.

Cherise coughed, opened her eyes, and flung her arms round Metal-Mutt. 'I love you!'

Metal-Mutt would have lain down and died for her right then and there.

The hug made the strange whirring noises between his ears even more intense: now it was like fifty wild bees trapped in his head. It didn't feel right: he didn't feel right, but he did feel wonderful.

'Good dog,' said Cherise. 'I love him, Mum. I want to keep him for

53

always and always.'

'He's a lovely dog,' said her mum. 'But he's so beautiful and clever, I'm afraid he must belong to someone. We can't keep him.'

Oh, yes you can! You can! thought Metal-Mutt, desperately. He rolled on his back and showed his underneath. Keep me! Please!

'He hasn't got a collar,' said Cherise, feeling round the dog's neck with her small hands. 'Can't we just take him home and see if anyone comes to find him?'

'Well . . .'

'Please, please!'

Please, please, begged Metal-Mutt silently. Take me home! No more CRUMMS!

10
A Real Home for Metal-Mutt

Cherise and her mum lived on the other side of the park, but to reach their house, they had to walk down Iydal Avenue.

Metal-Mutt began to tremble. What if the Crumms saw him?

'Poor boy, are you cold?' Cherise asked him.

Uh, oh, here was the Crumms' house! Metal-Mutt wanted to shrink into nothingness. I'm invisible, he told himself, pressing against Cherise. I'm invisible. Please let the Crumms be watching TV. Please. And the Crumms were so lazy, that's just what they were doing.

'I hope he doesn't run off,' said Cherise's mum. 'This is a busy road.'

Run away? thought Metal-Mutt, keeping his wet body touching Cherise. Run away? Me? I'd rather kiss a cat! I'd rather eat cold cabbage. I wish I was super-glued to the girl!

Cherise patted his head.

'What a good dog he is, Mum,' she said. 'He's staying really, really close.'

'He does seem like a nice fellow,' agreed her mum.

Oh, I am, I am, thought Metal-Mutt, desperately.

At last they reached Cherise's house.

Metal-Mutt shook off the river water before going inside so as not to make a mess.

It was a very nice home. It wasn't spotless, but it was clean and it had a cosy smell of hot ironing and honey.

Metal-Mutt cast his professional eye over the place. There were some magazines on the floor. Dust on the skirting board. A pile of crumpled clothes in a basket waiting to be ironed.

I suppose I'd better get started, he thought, but when he went over to the magazines, he couldn't lift them. His body just wouldn't work.

Before he could try again, Cherise brought him something to drink.

'I'm sorry we haven't got any dog food,' she said. 'Do you like warm milk?'

Do I like warm milk? Metal-Mutt wagged his tail. He lapped it up quickly.

OK, now better start on that ironing, he thought. They'll expect it done by supper time. But he couldn't move, his insides were hurting. He lay down on the floor, dog-tired.

'Poor thing,' said Cherise, stroking him. 'He's exhausted. He swam such a lot. He's wonderful. He's my hero.'

'I'll phone the RSPCA,' said Cherise's mum, 'and see if anyone's lost him.'

'Well his owners don't deserve him,' said Cherise. 'They haven't even given him a collar with a name on it.'

'True,' agreed her mum.

Metal-Mutt listened anxiously while Cherise's mum made the phone call. Nobody had reported a missing dog like Metal-Mutt.

Of course the Crumm family were far too lazy to contact the RSPCA. Perhaps they wouldn't even notice he was missing until they got hungry.

'So we can keep him then?'

said Cherise.

'For the moment,' said her mum.

'He'd protect us like a guard dog,' said Cherise. 'And I'd look after him and feed him and walk him every day, I promise.'

'We'll see,' said her mum. 'Now go and have a bath. You're still in wet clothes.'

Metal-Mutt followed Cherise upstairs to the bathroom and sat beside the bath. He was never going to leave this girl, ever.

When Cherise got soap in her eyes, Metal-Mutt quickly handed her the towel.

'What a clever dog!' cried Cherise. She looked deep into Metal-Mutt's eyes. 'You're special, aren't you?'

Metal-Mutt wagged his tail.

'It's OK, I just know you are,' said Cherise.

Metal-Mutt was the happiest dog in the world.

Cherise bought him a blue collar
and matching lead. She bought him a
dog basket with a green cushion. She
even made him a tartan jacket for
chilly weather.

Cherise did take him to the park
every day just like she said she would.
And she gave him a name: Hero.

Isn't that the best name ever?
thought Metal-Mutt, gazing at his new
name disc on his collar. Hero. Not just
boring Rover or Rex, but Hero. Life
was bliss.

One day when he was out in the park with Cherise, they bumped into Tom, the Junior Inventor.

'Metal-Mutt,' he cried, bending down to pat his head. 'Good to see you!'

'You can't have him back,' said Cherise, grabbing Metal-Mutt and holding him tight. 'He's my Hero.'

'Don't worry, I don't want him back. It's just that I knew him a long time ago,' said Tom. 'Tell me, does he do anything special?'

'Oh, yes,' said Cherise, 'lots. Don't you, Hero? He eats spiders. He sleeps on my bed. He lies on his back in the sun. He scratches his ear. He howls when I play the piano. He's very special.'

Tom winked slyly at Metal-Mutt.

'Great. He always was very special. I'm glad he's found you.' He stroked Metal-Mutt's head. 'What happened to the Crumms, eh?' he whispered.

Metal-Mutt wagged his tail and gave a little growl.

Who cared what happened to the Crumms?

After Metal-Mutt's insides got wet, he couldn't do the clever things he used to do. He couldn't wash up or bake or even clean windows. But sometimes, when Cherise was out at school, Metal-Mutt managed to pick up her toys and make her bed. Sometimes, when nobody was looking, he folded up her clothes neatly and put the lid back on the toothpaste. Nothing either too strenuous or too conspicuous.

'You're the best dog in the world,' Cherise told him. 'A really doggy dog.'

Metal-Mutt agreed. And real dogs don't do dishes, do they?